Engineering Wonders

SPACECRAFT

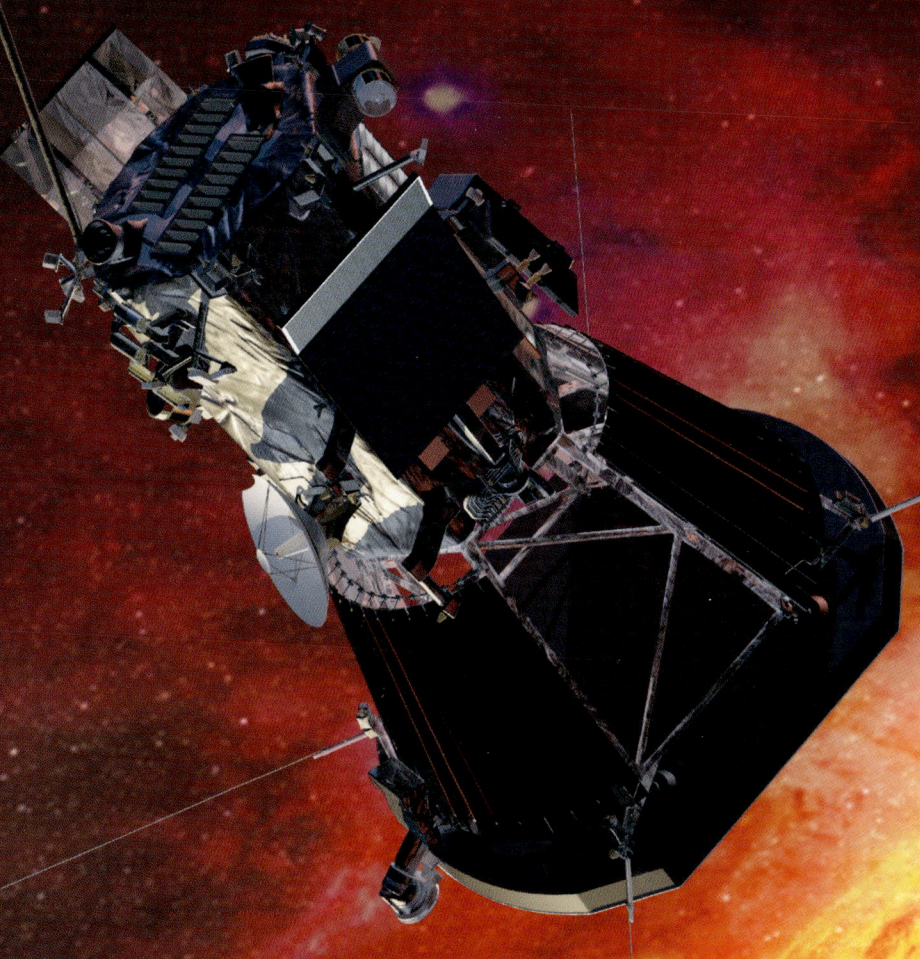

Clara MacCarald

rourkeeducationalmedia.com

Before, During, and After Reading Activities

Before Reading: Building Background Knowledge and Academic Vocabulary

"Before Reading" strategies activate prior knowledge and set a purpose for reading. Before reading a book, it is important to tap into what your child or students already know about the topic. This will help them develop their vocabulary and increase their reading comprehension.

Questions and activities to build background knowledge:
1. *Look at the cover of the book. What will this book be about?*
2. *What do you already know about the topic?*
3. *Let's study the Table of Contents. What will you learn about in the book's chapters?*
4. *What would you like to learn about this topic? Do you think you might learn about it from this book? Why or why not?*

Building Academic Vocabulary

Building academic vocabulary is critical to understanding subject content.
Assist your child or students to gain meaning of the following vocabulary words.

Content Area Vocabulary
Read the list. What do these words mean?

- asteroids
- atmosphere
- cargos
- commanders
- force
- friction
- galaxy
- kerosene
- probes
- radiation
- satellites
- vacuum

During Reading: Writing Component

"During Reading" strategies help to make connections, monitor understanding, generate questions, and stay focused.

1. *While reading, write in your reading journal any questions you have or anything you do not understand.*
2. *After completing each chapter, write a summary of the chapter in your reading journal.*
3. *While reading, make connections with the text and write them in your reading journal.*
   a) *Text to Self – What does this remind me of in my life? What were my feelings when I read this?*
   b) *Text to Text – What does this remind me of in another book I've read? How is this different from other books I've read?*
   c) *Text to World – What does this remind me of in the real world? Have I heard about this before? (News, current events, school, etc.…)*

After Reading: Comprehension and Extension Activity

"After Reading" strategies provide an opportunity to summarize, question, reflect, discuss, and respond to text. After reading the book, work on the following questions with your child or students to check their level of read comprehension and content mastery.

1. What are the things a crewed spacecraft must do to keep its crew alive? *(Summarize)*
2. Why did the governments of countries put the first astronauts in space rather than private companies? *(Infe*
3. How do rockets work in the vacuum of space? *(Asking Questions)*
4. If you could ride in a spacecraft to any place in the galaxy, where would you go? *(Text to Self Connection)*

Extension Activity

Build a rocket balloon! You'll need a deflated balloon, a plastic straw, and a rubber band. Push part of the straw into the mouth of the balloon. Use the rubber band to hold the straw in place. If you blow up the balloon throu the straw and let go, air will rush back out of the straw, pushing the balloon in the opposite direction. How doe move differently along the ground than a balloon without a straw? Try moving a toy boat by attaching your roc balloon to it with tape.

TABLE OF CONTENTS

The Final Frontier 4
History of Spacecraft 11
Lift Off! 19
Space Travel 24
Working in Space 32
The Future of Spacecraft 38
Timeline 44
Glossary 46
Index 47
Show What You Know 47
Further Reading 47
About the Author 48

First flown in 1985, the space shuttle Atlantis *was 122 feet (37 meters) long with a 78-foot (24-meter) wingspan.*

THE FINAL FRONTIER

On May 11, 2009, space shuttle *Atlantis* sat on a launchpad at Cape Canaveral, Florida. Inside, a crew of seven astronauts strapped down tight. The rockets started. Flames and clouds of smoke poured from the craft as it lifted off from Earth.

Space Shuttles
NASA built five space shuttles, which flew a total of 135 missions. Each held seven crew members. They carried **satellites** *and parts of the International Space Station into space. Two shuttles were destroyed. In 2011, NASA grounded the remaining shuttles.*

4

The ship sailed through the air, shedding its two rockets and fuel tank when they were no longer needed. It left the **atmosphere** and entered space. *Atlantis* began to orbit Earth. The crew had an important mission. They needed to repair the Hubble Space Telescope, which had been in space for almost 30 years.

Atlantis chased after Hubble and caught it two days later. *Atlantis* grabbed the telescope with a robotic arm. Linked, the two continued to orbit Earth together. Cameras on *Atlantis* took pictures of the telescope while astronauts suited up for a spacewalk.

Hubble's six batteries normally get their power from two solar panels that stretch from the telescope like wings.

The astronauts repaired parts on Hubble. They charged the telescope's batteries. They also added new parts, including scientific instruments and a device to help future missions capture Hubble more easily. After five spacewalks, the robot arm returned Hubble back into orbit. *Atlantis* returned to Earth.

> **Hubble Spies on the Universe**
> *On Earth, the atmosphere alters light coming from outer space. From orbit, Hubble can use its giant telescope to take much clearer images of the cosmos. Hubble has photographed monster black holes and studied distant planets.*

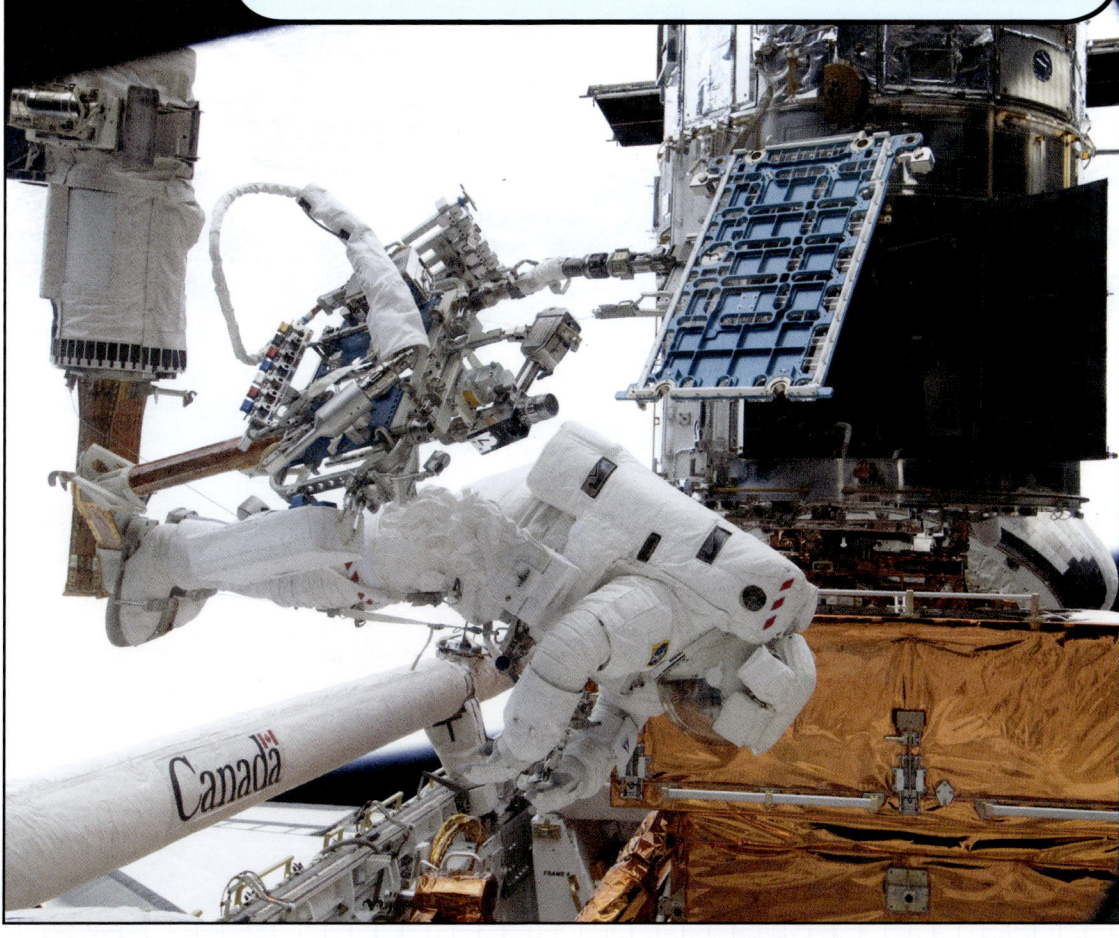

Since 1990, when the space shuttle Discovery *placed Hubble in space, astronauts have captured the telescope five times for repairs.*

Although very different, *Atlantis* and Hubble were both spacecraft. *Atlantis* carried a crew while Hubble was a robot, but they both traveled outside of Earth's atmosphere. Space presents many challenges, so engineers must design spacecraft to meet those challenges.

> **CubeSats: Tiny but Powerful**
> *CubeSats are tiny satellites. Many measure 3.9 inches (10 centimeters) on each side and weigh about 3 pounds (1.4 kilograms). CubeSats are cheap to make and easy to launch. Instruments onboard can transmit signals and record scientific information.*

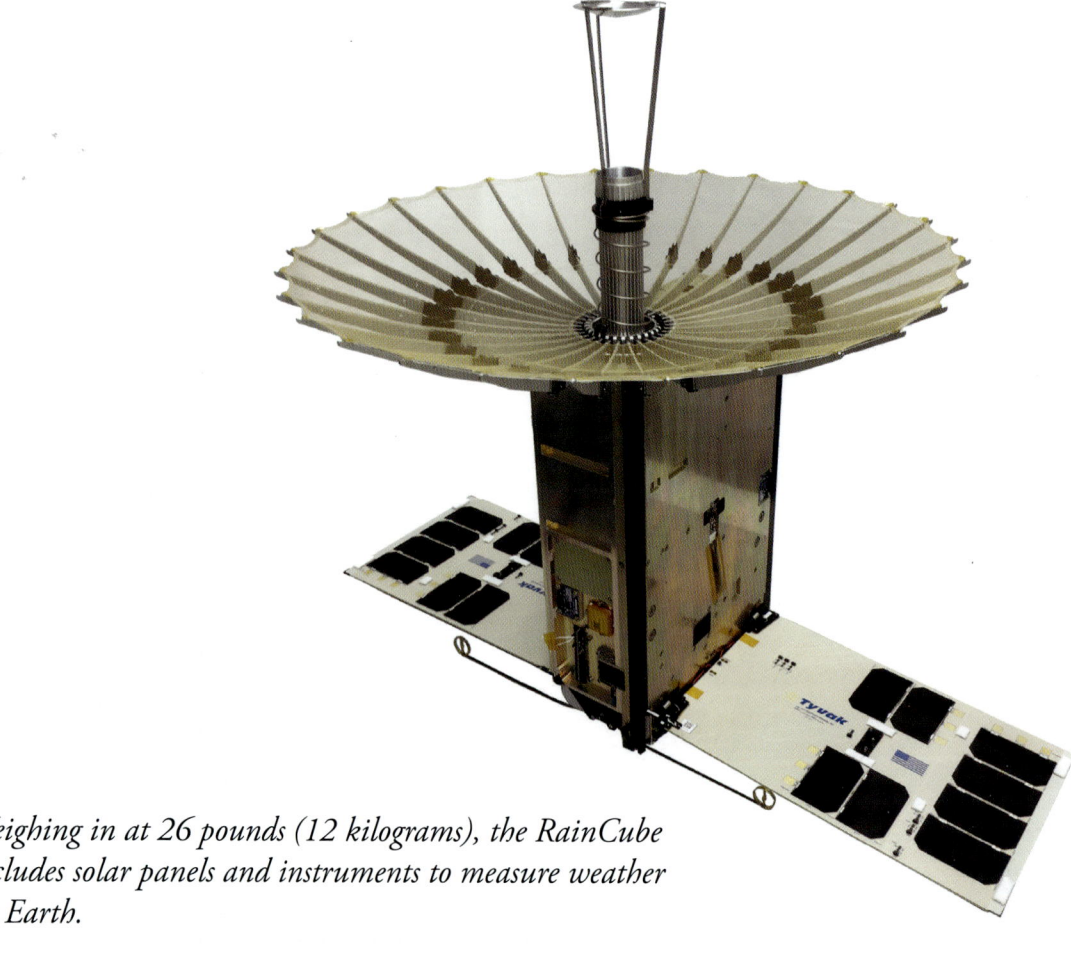

Weighing in at 26 pounds (12 kilograms), the RainCube includes solar panels and instruments to measure weather on Earth.

A spacecraft must escape Earth's atmosphere and travel through space. It must keep any passengers and crew alive. And it must have the equipment to successfully perform its mission. Humans have launched satellites, orbiters, space shuttles, and deep space **probes** into space. Some orbit above Earth's sky. Others sail toward other planets and even beyond the solar system.

The Cassini spacecraft explored Saturn, taking detailed photographs of the planet along with its moons. Cassini released a lander that in 2005 touched down on Titan, the largest of Saturn's moons.

9

Space Junk

Earth's orbit is becoming crowded. Millions of pieces of trash zoom above the atmosphere at high speeds, including abandoned spacecraft and broken parts. The junk isn't just ugly—it's also dangerous. Some pieces have hit space shuttles and satellites.

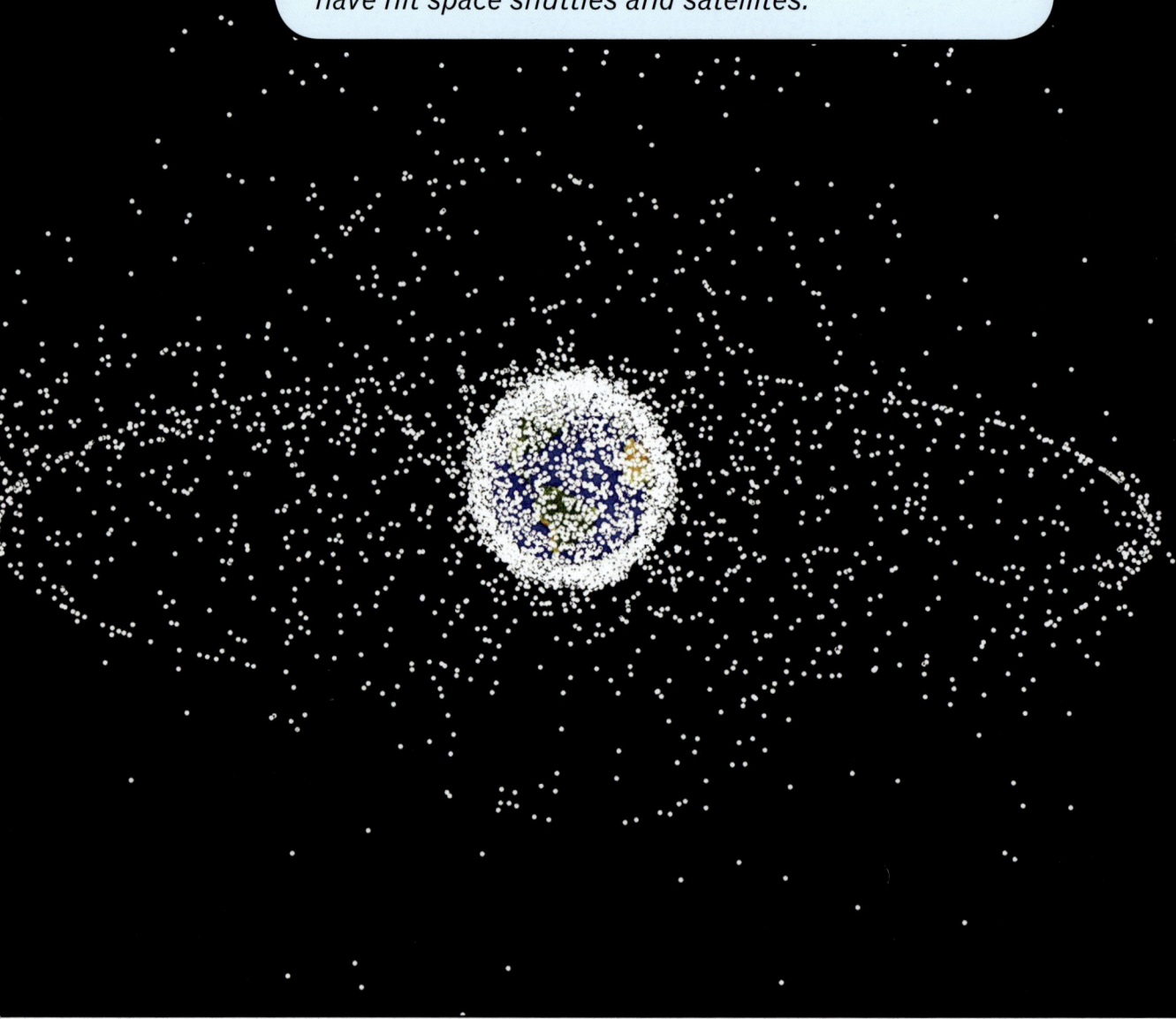

Organizations on the ground track thousands of the larger pieces of space junk. Sometimes spacecraft must change course to avoid a collision.

HISTORY OF SPACECRAFT

By the 13th century, the Chinese had invented rockets powered by gunpowder. In the early 20th century, Dr. Robert Hutchings Goddard developed the first rocket that used liquid fuel. Goddard realized the potential for such a rocket to reach the moon. During World War II (1939–1945), German rockets used liquid fuel to send missiles over long distances.

In 1926, Dr. Robert Hutchings Goddard launched the first rocket to use liquid fuel, although it only rose up 41 feet (12 meters) into the air.

After the war ended, researchers aimed for space. On October 4, 1957, the Soviet Union surprised its rival, the United States, by launching *Sputnik 1*. Though *Sputnik* only stayed in orbit a short time, it was the first human-made satellite. This achievement started the Space Race, a competition between the Soviets and the Americans.

> **Origins of NASA**
> In 1915, the U.S. Congress formed an organization named NACA to help develop plane technology. After World War II, the group worked on missiles and spacecraft. On October 1, 1958, a year after Sputnik launched, NASA replaced NACA.

Although NACA was originally tasked with overseeing the work of other groups instead of its own, NACA opened its first research lab in 1920.

At first, the Soviets maintained their lead. In November, the Soviets launched a dog. Engineers created a spacecraft which could keep the dog alive by controlling the air and temperature inside a small cabin. On April 12, 1961, Yuri Gagarin became the first human to reach space.

Yuri Gagarin's record-breaking flight around Earth took 108 minutes to complete. On his return to Earth, he abandoned the spacecraft and used a parachute to land safely on the ground.

> **Human Computers**
> In the early years, humans calculated flight paths for spacecraft at NASA. Most were women. Many were African American, including Katherine Johnson. In 1962, Johnson checked the numbers for John Glenn's spaceflight, the first full orbit made by an American.

Katherine Johnson's work on space flights led to many honors and awards, including the Presidential Medal of Freedom presented by President Barack Obama on November 24, 2015.

The United States scrambled to catch up. The first American arrived in space soon after Gagarin made his flight. The United States eventually won the Space Race by landing humans on the moon on July 20, 1969.

The Saturn V, *the rocket which launched the first astronauts to the moon, was 363 feet (110 meters) tall and could lift 130 tons (118,000 kilograms) to space.*

In 1975, an Apollo spacecraft from the United States met a Soyuz spacecraft from the Soviet Union in orbit. The **commanders** shook hands in space. The two rivals worked together from that point on.

> ### Live from the Moon
> *The historic trip to the moon began with a rocket launch watched by millions. Neil Armstrong steered past boulders to bring a lander down safely. As Armstrong took the first moon walk, people on Earth watched on live television.*

When the American and Russian spacecrafts joined, the crews gave each other gifts including their national flags. The two nations have worked together in space ever since.

Both robot and crewed spacecraft continued to reach new heights. America's *Pioneer 10* reached the outer solar system in 1973. In 1976, American landers touched down on Martian soil. In 1981, NASA launched the first space shuttle. It could bring a crew to space and land them back on a runway.

The *Viking 1* spacecraft launched from Cape Canaveral and traveled for about 11 months before arriving at Mars. Its lander became the first to successfully touch down on the surface on June 20, 1976.

Tragedies in Space Travel
A Soviet astronaut crashed in 1967, becoming the first human to die during space travel. In 1971, three Soviets died in space. The space shuttle Challenger exploded in 1986 while space shuttle Columbia broke up in 2003, killing 14 people altogether.

When space shuttle Columbia *launched on January 16, 2003, a bit of foam broke off its tank and damaged one wing. The damage doomed the shuttle when it tried to land 16 days later.*

LIFT OFF!

Any mission begins by reaching space. Reaching space requires fighting against Earth's gravity. Engineers use lighter metals such as aluminum and aluminum alloys to reduce the weight of spacecraft and launch vehicles. Still, liftoff takes a lot of fuel, more than a spacecraft uses to move through space.

Space shuttles launched with four parts: the spacecraft orbiter, two rocket boosters using solid fuel, and an external fuel tank with liquid fuel to supply the main engine. The tank held 535,000 gallons (2,025,000 liters).

Once the spacecraft has escaped the atmosphere, it doesn't need to carry all of the rockets and fuel tanks it used to lift off. Most spacecraft are carried to space by a launch vehicle. The launch vehicle lifts off using stages. Stages are special kinds of rockets. They break away from the spacecraft after they run out of fuel. The stages crash-land somewhere safe.

Some rocket stages are meant to be recovered, such as the first stage of the Ares 1-X. *NASA intended to use* Ares 1 *rockets to launch astronauts to space after they grounded the space shuttle, but the government canceled the Ares program.*

Liquid Gases

Hydrogen and oxygen occur as gases on Earth, but they become liquids at extremely low temperatures. Oxygen does so at minus-297 degrees Fahrenheit (-183 degrees Celsius). Hydrogen needs to be even colder: minus-423 degrees Fahrenheit (-253 degrees Celsius).

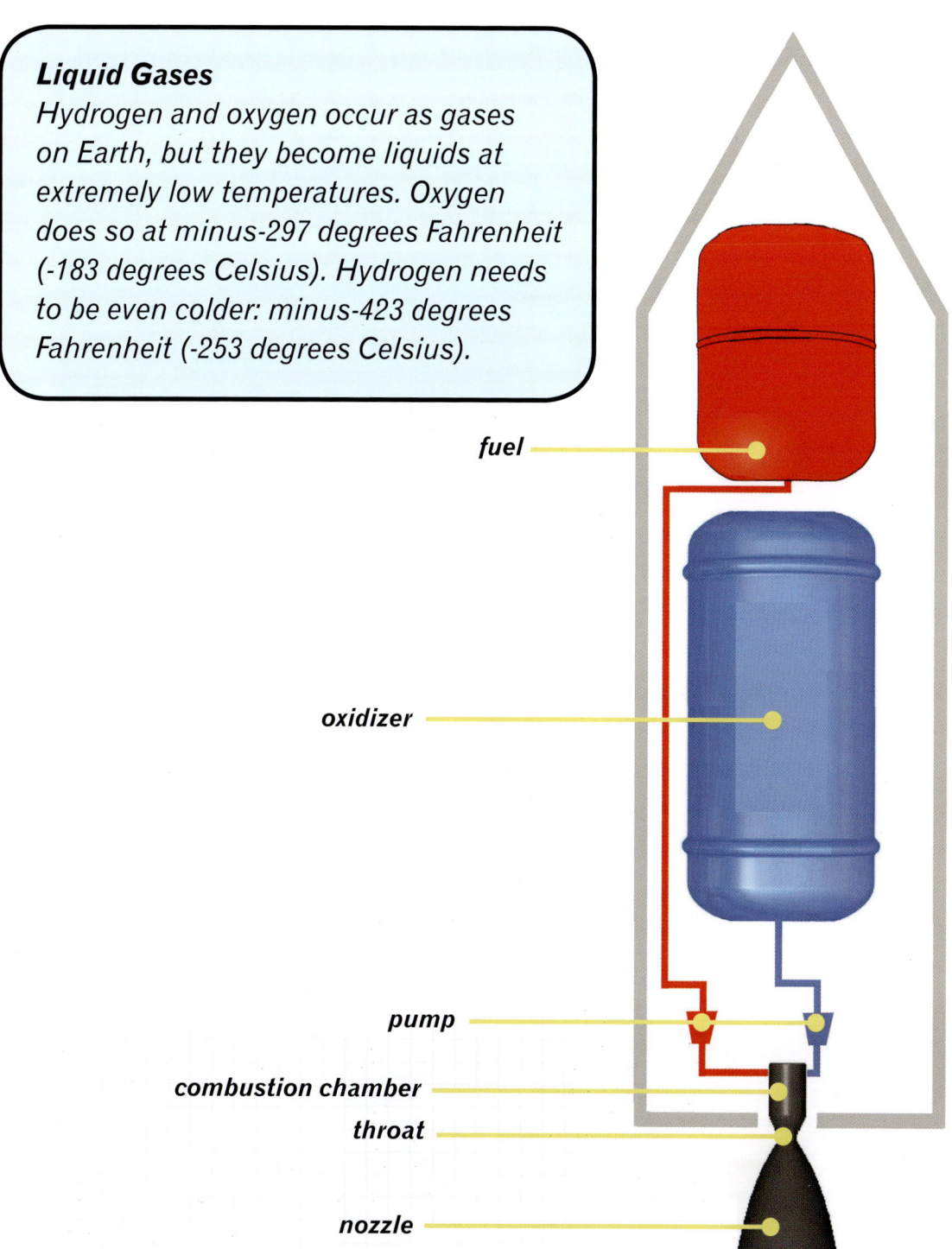

Rockets make power by burning fuel. Different rockets use different types of fuel. Some combine **kerosene** with liquid oxygen, causing it to burn. Other rockets combine liquid hydrogen with liquid oxygen. Combining the two not only makes an explosion—it also makes water.

If the liquid fuels get too hot before being used, they could boil off or explode. Engineers must design insulated tanks which carry the fuel safely. The tanks also keep the liquid fuels apart, pumping them together carefully when the engines are ready to go.

Once it climbed to 28 miles (45 kilometers) in the sky, the space shuttle released its solid rocket boosters. The tank jettisoned about 70 miles (113 kilometers) above Earth and was the only part not reused.

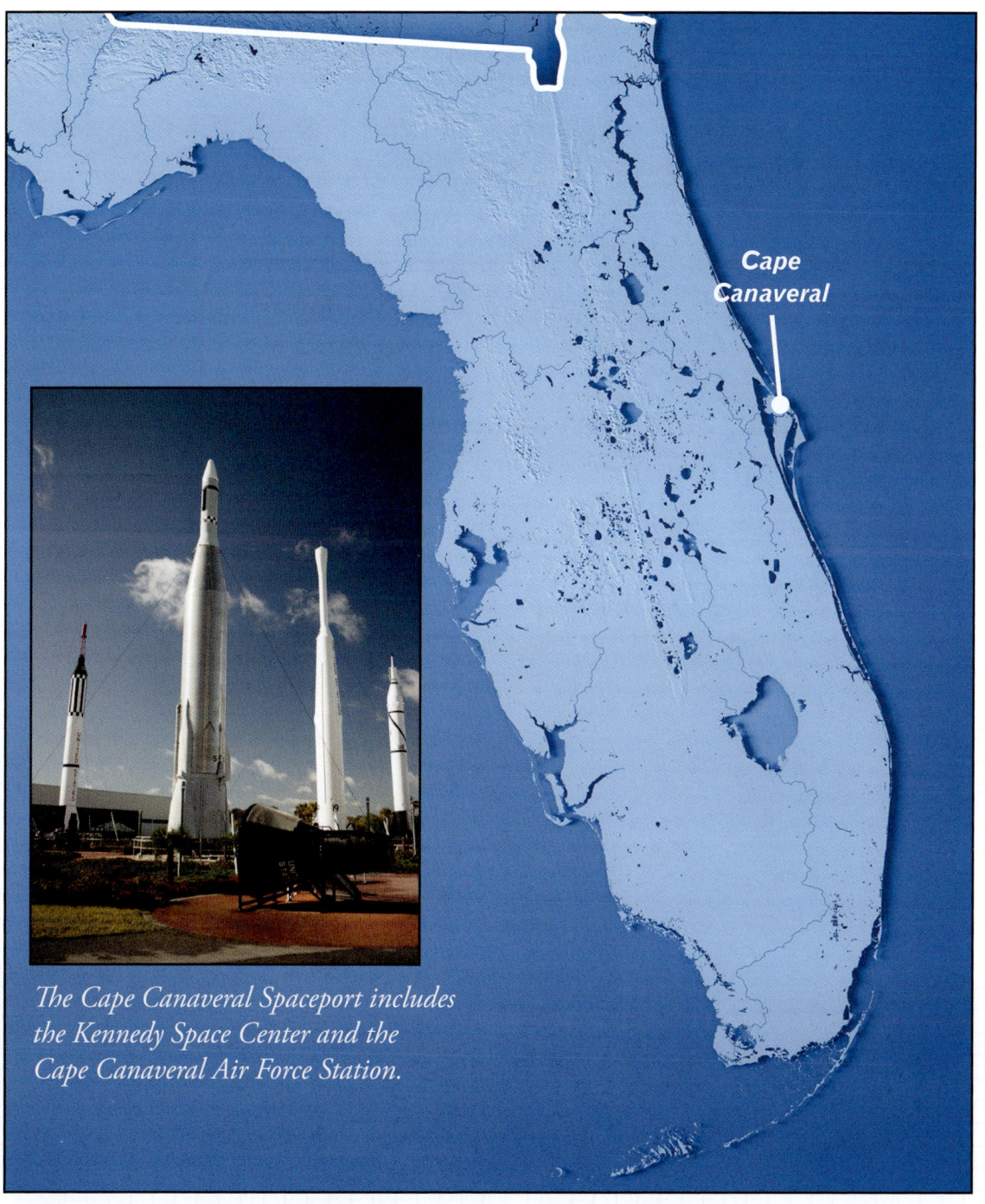

The Cape Canaveral Spaceport includes the Kennedy Space Center and the Cape Canaveral Air Force Station.

Many missions launch from sites on land. NASA uses several launch sites, including a famous one at Cape Canaveral, Florida. Other countries around the world have launch sites. Some missions launch from ships. A few launch from planes. By hitching a ride high into the air, the launch vehicle escapes the greatest pull of gravity near the surface, which means it can use less fuel.

SPACE TRAVEL

Once a spacecraft reaches space, it must travel to its target. Many spacecraft catch a ride on a larger spacecraft. Probes and landers might be shuttled across the solar system. At some point, they break free to travel on their own.

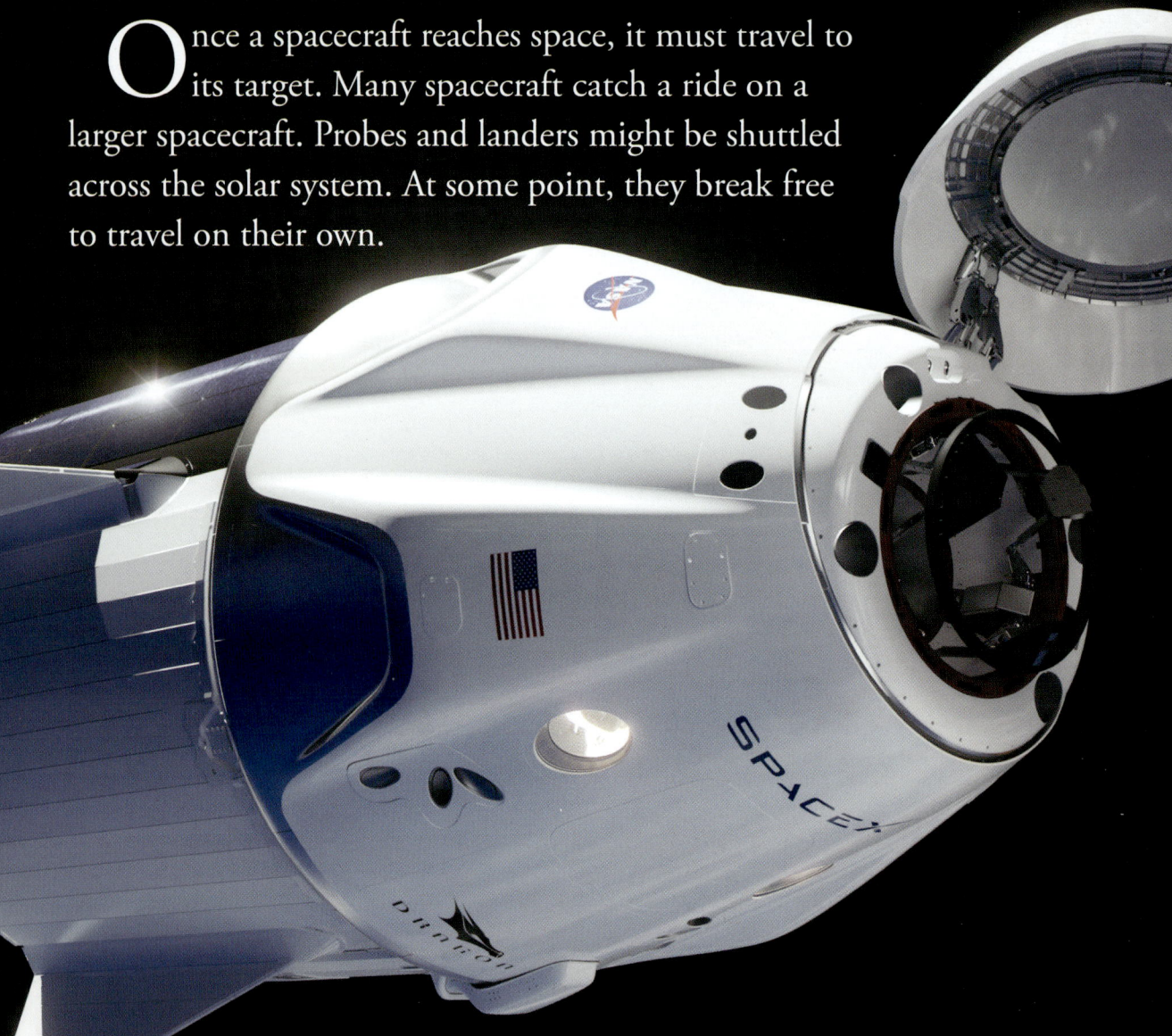

The SpaceX Dragon *has taken supplies to the International Space Station and returned things to Earth. NASA hopes to fly astronauts on the* Crew Dragon *sometime in 2019.*

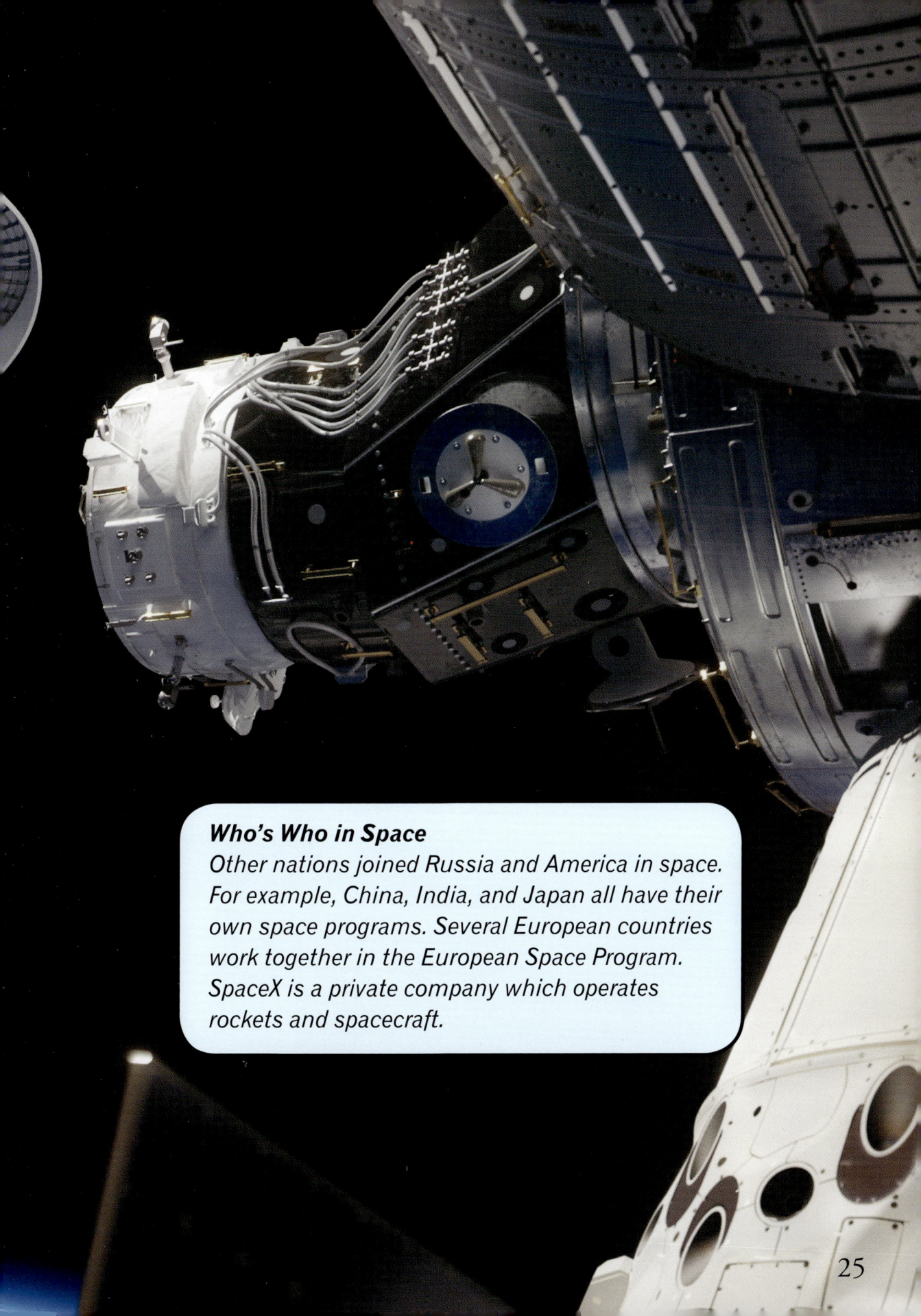

Who's Who in Space
Other nations joined Russia and America in space. For example, China, India, and Japan all have their own space programs. Several European countries work together in the European Space Program. SpaceX is a private company which operates rockets and spacecraft.

A spacecraft always orbits something. That something may be Earth, the sun, or the **galaxy** itself. To stay in Earth's orbit, an object must travel about 17,400 miles (28,000 kilometers) per hour. If it moves too slowly, gravity will cause the object to fall. If it goes too fast, the object will break free of Earth's gravity.

Since the last mission to the moon in 1972, astronauts have not traveled farther than low Earth orbit. Objects in low Earth orbits stay within the first 200 miles (322 kilometers) of space beyond Earth's atmosphere. They take about 90 minutes to travel fully around the globe.

Some spacecraft stay in the orbit where they were placed. Most need to move. But how do vehicles move in space? Ordinary planes have wings, which catch a lift from air pressure. Space has very low or no air pressure.

> **Running on Atoms**
> The Dawn spacecraft moves using an ion stream. Dawn's engine gives an electrical charge to gas atoms, which makes them ions. By releasing these ions at high speeds, the engine pushes the spacecraft forward.

After launching in 2007, Dawn *traveled to the asteroid belt between Mars and Jupiter. The spacecraft first visited Vesta, an asteroid, and then Ceres, a dwarf planet measuring about 590 miles (950 kilometers) across.*

Rocket Engine Thrust

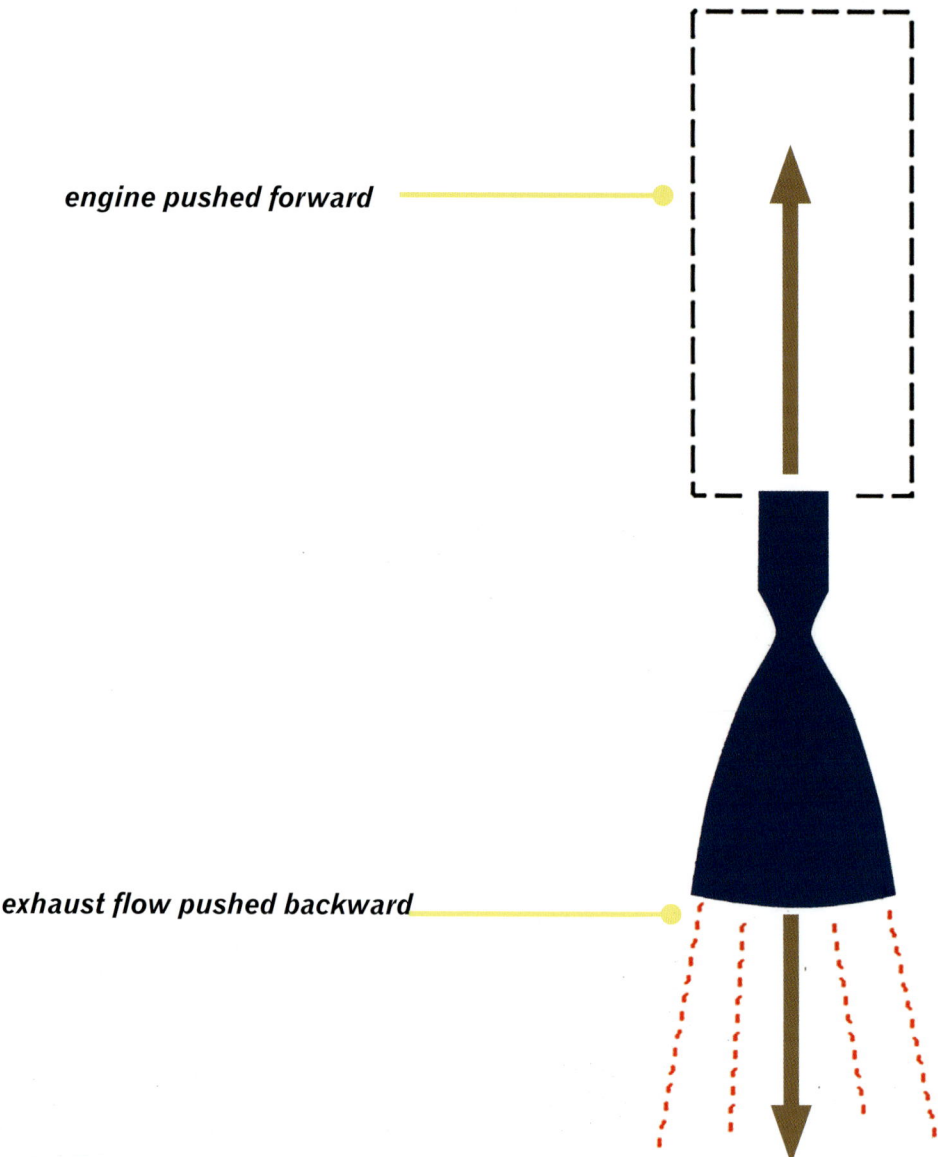

Rockets work without air pressure because of Newton's third law of motion. The law says that any action has an equal and opposite reaction. Rocket exhaust creates a **force** in one direction. The opposite force moves the vehicle, similar to a balloon letting out air. Not all spacecraft need rockets to move. For example, Hubble spins its wheels in one direction, producing a force in the opposite direction.

NEWTON'S LAWS OF MOTION

First law of motion
Law of inertia
An object that is not moving will not move until a force makes it move. An object that is moving will continue to move at a constant speed and direction until a force causes it to change.

Second law of motion
F=ma
The force of an object equals its mass times its acceleration. Newton's second law is a formula. If force equals mass times acceleration, then acceleration equals force divided by mass. When the formula is written this way, it explains that an object's speed, or velocity, will depend on its mass and the force that is applied to it.

Third law of motion
Law of action and reaction
For every action there is an equal and opposite reaction.

All of Newton's laws help scientists and engineers understand how planes, rockets, and spacecraft move both in the atmosphere and in space.

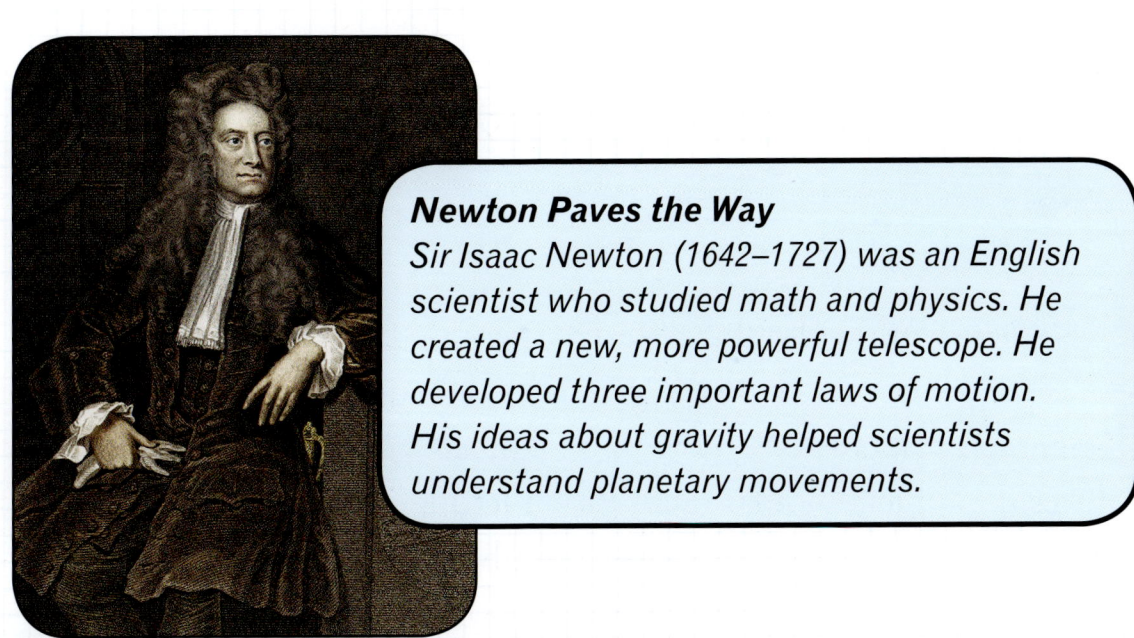

Newton Paves the Way
Sir Isaac Newton (1642–1727) was an English scientist who studied math and physics. He created a new, more powerful telescope. He developed three important laws of motion. His ideas about gravity helped scientists understand planetary movements.

By speeding up, some spacecraft can use Earth's gravity like a slingshot. They fling themselves toward distant objects in the solar system. To orbit a different planet, the spacecraft must slow enough to be captured by the planet's gravity. A spacecraft which flies close to a planet without entering orbit will either speed up or slow down.

Planet Hopping
In 1977, Voyagers 1 and 2 left Earth to explore the planets. They used Jupiter's gravity to speed up toward Saturn. From Saturn, they hopped to Uranus and Neptune. Both spacecraft were headed out of the solar system in 2018.

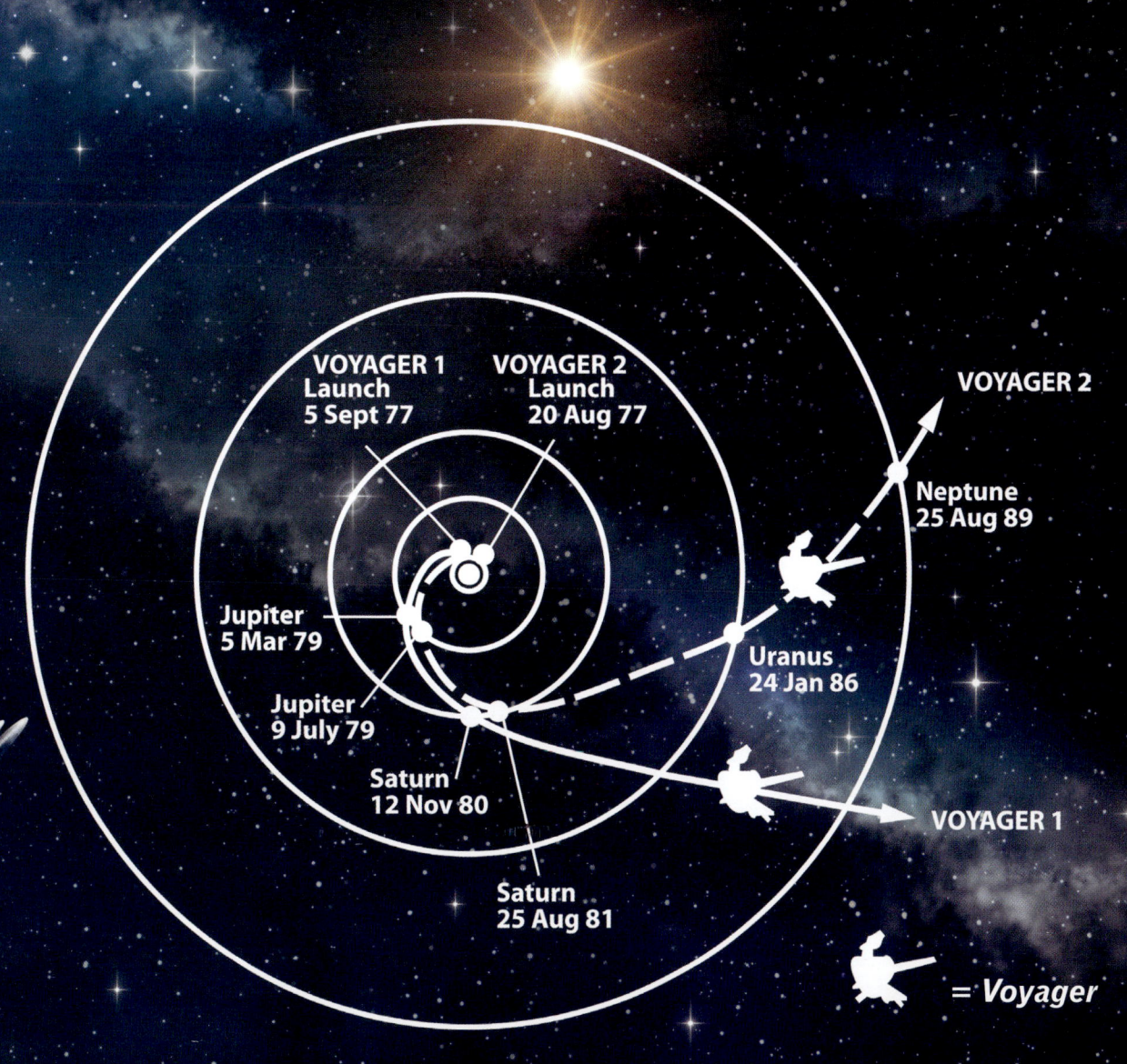

Using Jupiter's gravity, Voyagers 1 and 2 sped up away from the sun by about 35,700 miles per hour (57,500 kilometers per hour). On its entire trip from Earth to Neptune, Voyager 2 traveled about 30,000 miles (48,000 kilometers) per gallon (3.8 liters) of fuel.

WORKING IN SPACE

Once the spacecraft arrives at its destination, there's work to be done. The design of a spacecraft depends on its mission. A spacecraft might need to run experiments, make scientific observations, or transmit signals for other devices. Some spacecraft visit planets, moons, comets, or **asteroids**. They may fly by, enter orbit, or land on an object.

A freezer on the International Space Station stays as low as -80 degrees Celsius (-112 degrees Fahrenheit) to preserve biological samples, including blood or other material taken from the crew for testing.

Spacecraft can carry different kinds of scientific instruments. They need to protect these instruments from extreme temperature and **radiation**. Some instruments study things they touch, such as dust in space. Others study distant objects by taking measurements or pictures. Spacecraft have communication devices to send information back to people on the ground.

> **Radiation in Space**
> *Radiation is a kind of energy. It moves as rays, waves, or extremely tiny particles. It can damage both equipment and living things. Earth's magnetic field protects the planet from radiation from the sun and from outside the solar system.*

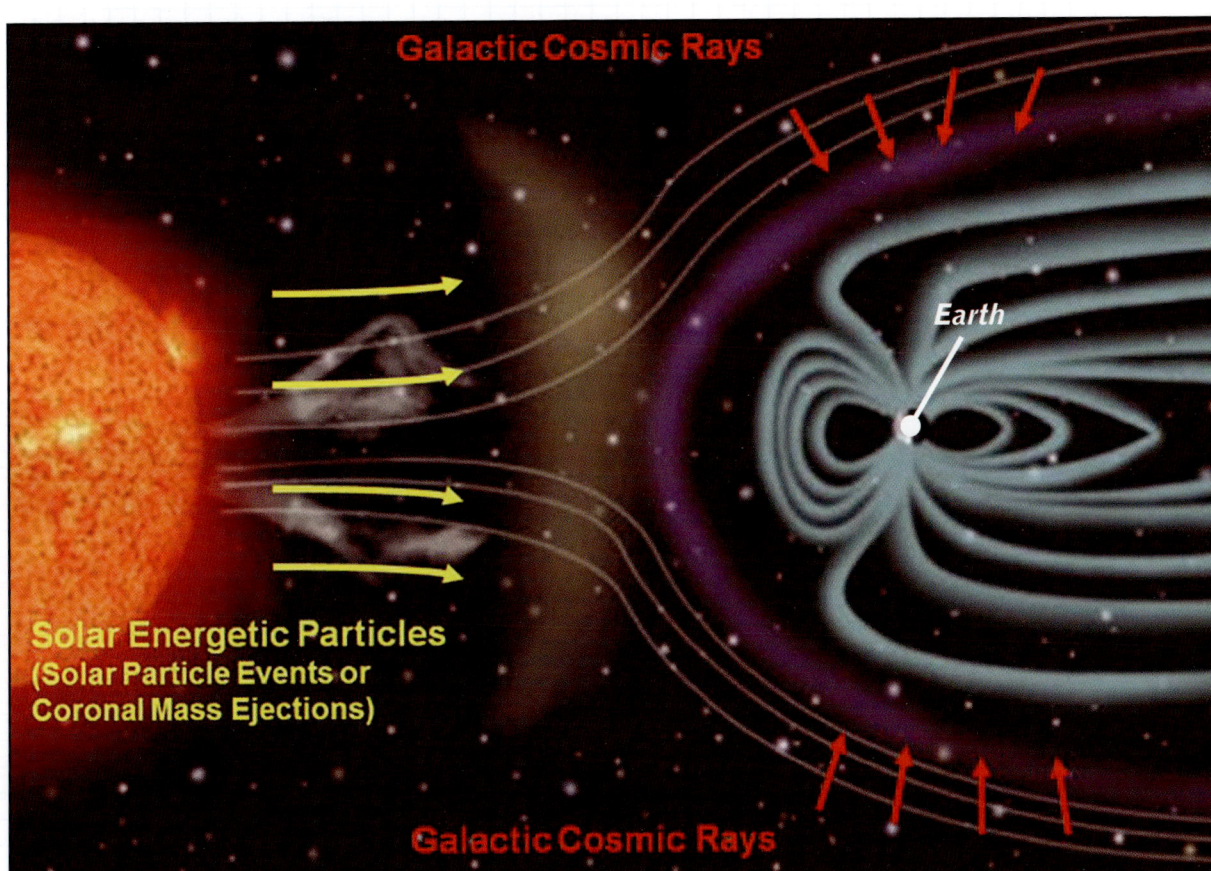

When the sun flares, solar radiation can travel the 93 million miles (150 million kilometers) to Earth in 30 minutes or less. Cosmic rays can move almost as fast as light, which travels about 186,000 miles (300,000 kilometers) per second.

Humans pose special challenges for engineers designing spacecraft. A crew needs oxygen, air pressure, safe temperatures, food, and water. Spacecraft systems must deal with the carbon dioxide and other waste that living creatures produce. Gym space and equipment allow astronauts to exercise.

Astronauts can't lift weights when everything is weightless, but a machine on the International Space Station simulates lifting up to 600 pounds (272 kilograms).

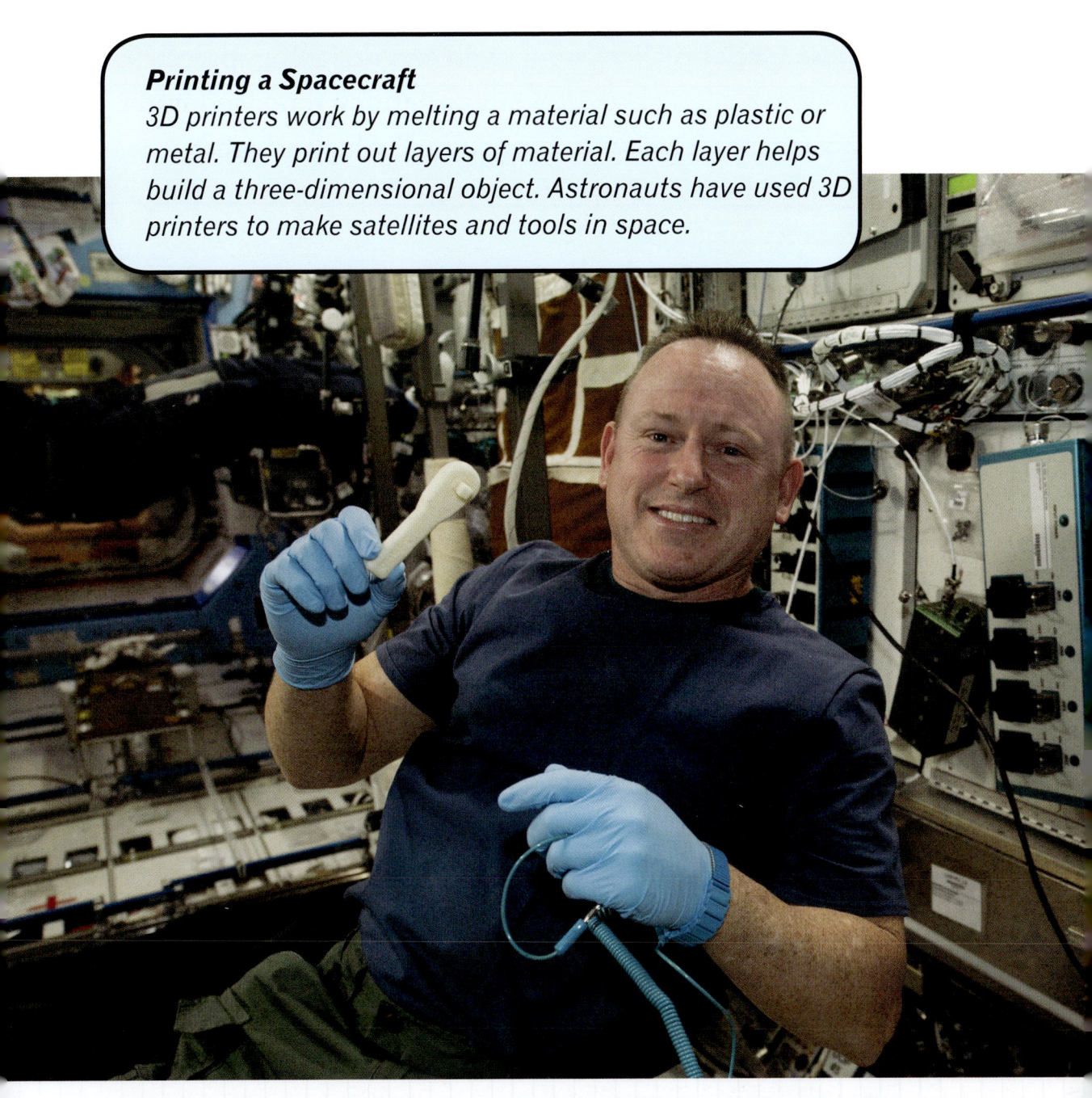

> ### *Printing a Spacecraft*
> 3D printers work by melting a material such as plastic or metal. They print out layers of material. Each layer helps build a three-dimensional object. Astronauts have used 3D printers to make satellites and tools in space.

Printers on the International Space Station have made objects such as wrenches, CubeSat parts, and small radiation shields.

Sometimes astronauts must walk outside the spacecraft to run an experiment or make repairs. They put on a special suit to survive in the deadly **vacuum** of space. Air locks allow astronauts to leave and enter the spacecraft without losing all the air inside the craft.

A crewed spacecraft needs to bring its astronauts home. The spacecraft first slows in order to drop out of Earth's orbit. The craft enters the atmosphere. **Friction** creates extremely high temperatures. A heat shield keeps the craft from burning up. Parachutes and rockets slow the craft down further.

NASA is developing the Orion *spacecraft to take crews on missions into deep space. In tests,* Orion *will hit the atmosphere at 20,000 miles per hour (32,000 kilometers per hour) to return to Earth.*

Some robot spacecraft are not meant to be recovered. Once they complete their mission, they might lose power and stay in orbit as space junk. Small craft might burn up in a planet's atmosphere or crash-land.

Measuring 10 feet (three meters) across and traveling at about 8,750 miles per hour (14,080 kilometers) per hour), Messenger probably made a crater 52 feet (16 meters) wide when it crashed into Mercury.

First Rock from the Sun
From 2011 to 2015, the Messenger *spacecraft orbited Mercury, the planet closest to the sun.* Messenger *used a ceramic shield to protect its instruments from the extremely hot sunlight. After running out of fuel,* Messenger *crashed into Mercury.*

THE FUTURE OF SPACECRAFT

New means of travel may someday help spacecraft do more with less fuel. One idea is to go nuclear. Researchers are working on nuclear-powered rockets. A nuclear reaction would heat liquid hydrogen to a boil. Hydrogen gas would stream away, pushing the spacecraft along.

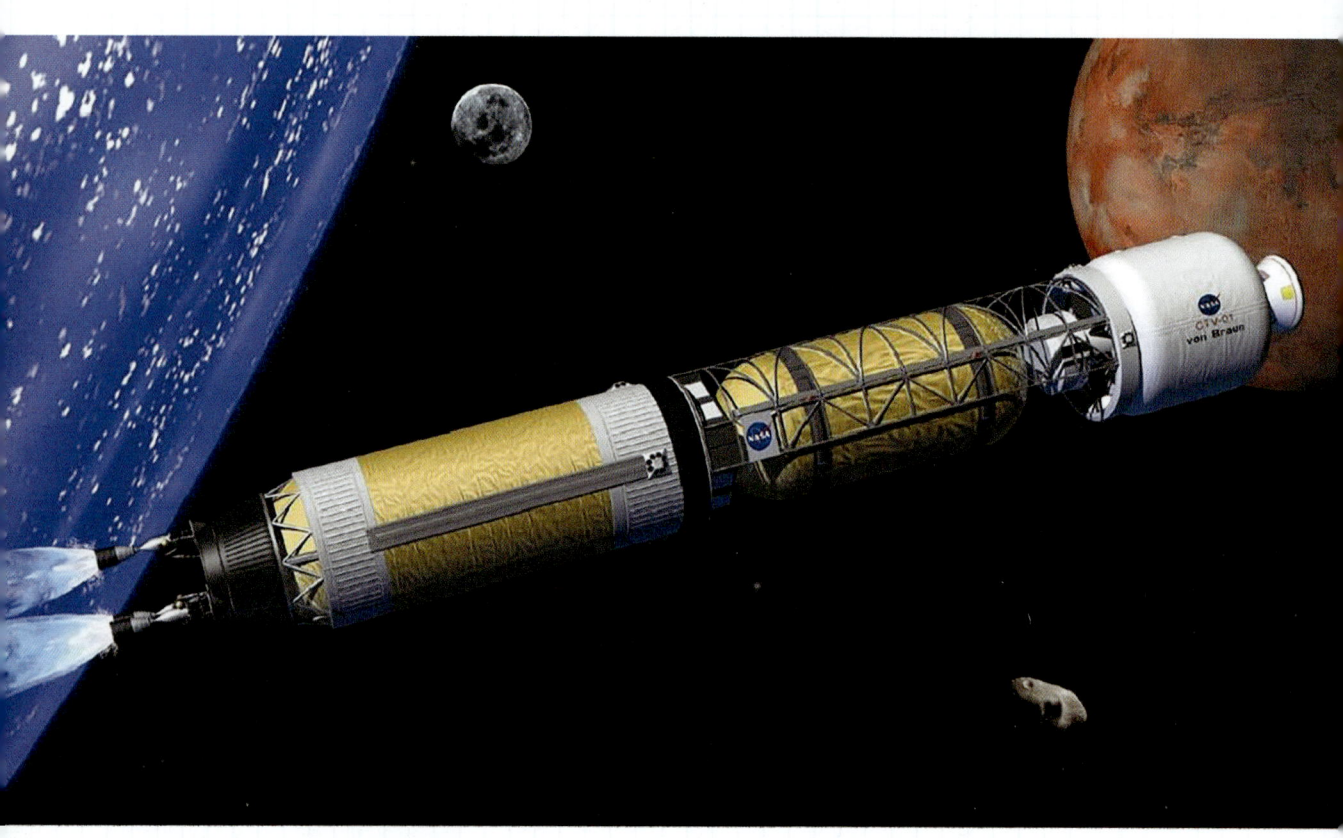

Scientists first looked at using nuclear rockets in the 1950s and 60s. Using a spacecraft which launches with regular fuel and moves through space with nuclear power could cut the trip to Mars in half.

Engineers may create technologies in the future which power spacecraft without the craft needing to carry fuel. Solar sails are huge but very thin. They use the pressure of sunlight itself to move a spacecraft. A different kind of sail could be powered by lasers operated on Earth.

The *Ikaros* spacecraft, launched by the Japanese Space Agency, opened up the first successful solar sail in space in 2010. The sail was 46 feet (14 meters) wide, but others in the works are even larger.

Engineers at NASA are working on the Space Launch System. Using powerful rockets, the system will send even larger **cargos** to the moon and beyond. NASA has its sights set on Mars.

> **Living in Low Gravity**
> *Low gravity affects the health of astronauts. While in space, astronauts lose minerals from their bones. Their muscles and lungs weaken. Fluids build up in the wrong places. Astronauts can fight some of these problems with exercise and special clothing.*

But taking humans to Mars will be a challenge. Even when Mars and Earth are at their closest, they are still 34.8 million miles (55 million kilometers) apart. The trip to Mars could take about nine months. That's a long time to be in space. Radiation and weightlessness will threaten the health of the crew.

Two companies, Boeing and SpaceX, have each created a new type of spacesuit using special material to make it lighter and easier to move in.

Longer missions will require new technologies. Faster spacecraft could limit the time humans spend in space. Plants could provide oxygen and purify water. Once the astronauts arrive in orbit around Mars, engineers will need to find a way to land them safely on the surface.

Colonists on Mars will probably grow crops to produce both food and oxygen. Astronauts have already grown food plants on the International Space Station.

The future will see spacecraft going to new places and doing new things. Scientists will learn more about our solar system, the universe, and even Earth. On some of those missions, human crews will travel farther than anyone has ever gone before.

Why Mars?
Humans may colonize Mars before the end of the century. Why the Red Planet? It's near Earth, and close enough to the sun to use solar power. Scientists have found ice on Mars, which might provide a source of water.

43

TIMELINE

1957 The Soviet Union successfully reachs space with *Sputnik 1*, the first human-made satellite.

1959 The Soviets crash into the moon with *Luna 2*, a probe carrying no rockets but several scientific instruments.

1961 Alan Shepard becomes the first American in space.

1969 Neil Armstrong becomes the first human to walk on the moon, joined soon afterward by Buzz Aldrin. Four days later, they and Michael Collins, who stayed in moon orbit rather than landing, splash down near Hawaii.

1972 *Pioneer 10* becomes the first spacecraft to enter the asteroid belt between Mars and Jupiter.

1976   *Viking 1* lands on Mars, which it will explore for the next six years. Earlier missions crashed or worked for less than a minute.

1981   NASA launches the first space shuttle into orbit.

1990   The space shuttle *Discovery* places the Hubble Space Telescope into orbit.

2012   NASA lands the *Curiosity* rover on Mars.

2018   NASA launches the *Parker Solar* Probe, which aims to touch the sun's atmosphere.

As early as 2023, astronauts may leave Earth's low orbit on an Orion *spacecraft to circle around the moon.*

GLOSSARY

asteroids (AS-tuh-roids): rocky objects in orbit around the sun

atmosphere (AT-muhs-feer): the gases surrounding a planet

cargos (KAHR-gohs): sets of goods carried by a vehicle such as a spacecraft

commanders (kuh-MAN-durs): the people in charge of missions

force (fors): energy which changes an object's movement or shape

friction (FRIK-shuhn): the action of one object or substance rubbing against another, which produces energy

galaxy (GAL-uhk-see): a system of billions of stars and planets

kerosene (KER-uh-seen): a colorless liquid fuel made by refining petroleum

probes (prohbs): devices used to explore or study something

radiation (ray-dee-AY-shuhn): energy which travels in the form of waves, rays, or particles

satellites (SAT-uh-lites): objects which orbit a planet or a moon

vacuum (VAK-yoom): an area with no air or gas

INDEX

Cape Canaveral, Florida 4, 23
Earth 4, 5, 6, 7, 8, 9, 10, 16, 19, 24, 26, 30, 33, 36, 39, 41, 43
Hubble Space Telescope 5, 6, 7, 8, 28
Mars 40, 41, 42, 43
moon 11, 15, 16, 40
NASA 4, 12, 14, 17, 23, 24, 36, 40
rocket(s) 4, 5, 11, 20, 21, 25, 28, 36, 38, 40
Soviet Union 12, 16
space shuttle 17, 18, 19, 22
sun 26, 33, 37, 43
United States 12, 15, 16

SHOW WHAT YOU KNOW

1. Who won the Space Race and how did they win?
2. Why did the space shuttle *Atlantis* capture the Hubble Space Telescope in 2009?
3. What happens when an object orbiting a planet moves too slowly?
4. Why do engineers make spacecraft weigh as little as possible?
5. What is space junk?

FURTHER READING

McMahon, Peter, *The Space Adventurer's Guide: Your Passport to the Coolest Things to See and Do in the Universe*, Kids Can Press, 2018.

Olson, Tod, *Lost in Outer Space: The Incredible Journey of Apollo 13*, Scholastic, 2017.

Sabol, Stephanie, *Where Is Our Solar System?* Penguin Workshop, 2018.

ABOUT THE AUTHOR

Clara MacCarald is a writer with a master's degree in biology. She lives with her family in an off-grid house nestled in the forests of central New York. When not parenting her daughter, she spends her time writing nonfiction books for kids.

Meet The Author!
www.meetREMauthors.com

© 2019 Rourke Educational Media

All rights reserved. No part of this book may be reproduced or utilized in any form or by any means, electronic or mechanical including photocopying, recording, or by any information storage and retrieval system without permission in writing from the publisher.

www.rourkeeducationalmedia.com

PHOTO CREDITS: Cover and title page: ©NASA, Pg 1-48 ©Page Art; Pg 3, 4, 6, 7, 8, 9, 10, 11, 12, 13, 14, 15, 16, 17, 18, 19, 22, 26, 31, 32, 33, 34, 35, 36, 37, 38, 39, 42, 44 ©NASA; Pg 20 ©United Space Alliance; Pg 21 ©Nwbeeson - wiki; Pg 23 ©FrankRamspott; Pg 23 ©Pgiam; Pg 24 ©SpaceX; Pg 27 ©NASA/JPL-Caltech; Pg 29 ©duncan1890; Pg 30 ©titoOnz; Pg 40 ©Tokarsky; Pg 41 ©Boeing

Edited by: Keli Sipperley
Cover design by: Rhea Magaro-Wallace
Interior design by: Kathy Walsh

Library of Congress PCN Data

Spacecraft / Clara MacCarald
(Engineering Wonders)
ISBN 978-1-64369-049-0 (hard cover)(alk.paper)
ISBN 978-1-64369-089-6 (soft cover)
ISBN 978-1-64369-196-1 (e-Book)
Library of Congress Control Number: 2018955985
Rourke Educational Media
Printed in the United States of America, North Mankato, Minnesota